Dragons from Mars

By Deborah Aronson

Illustrated by Colin Jack

HARPER

An Imprint of HarperCollinsPublishers

Dragons from Mars

Text copyright © 2016 by Deborah Aronson

Illustrations copyright © 2016 by Colin Jack

Library of Congress Cataloging-in-Publication Data

Aronson, Deborah, author.

Dragons from Mars / by Deborah Aronson ; illustrated by Colin Jack. — First edition.

pages cm

Summary: Nathaniel loves dragons and wonders if any live on Mars, so he sends an email invitation and is surprised when Molly and Fred Dragon come to stay at his house.

ISBN 978-0-06-236850-8 (hardcover)

[1. Stories in rhyme. 2. Dragons—Fiction. 3. Extraterrestrial beings—Fiction.] I. Jack, Colin, illustrator. II. Title.

PZ8.3.A6815Dr 2016   2015018267

[E]—dc23   CIP

                                                                                                      AC

The artist used Photoshop and Sketchbook Pro to create the digital illustrations for this book.

Typography by Dana Fritts

16 17 18 19 20 SCP 10 9 8 7 6 5 4 3 2 1

First Edition

With love to Peter,
my best and dearest captive audience

—D.A.

For G. and E.
Love, Dad

—C. J.

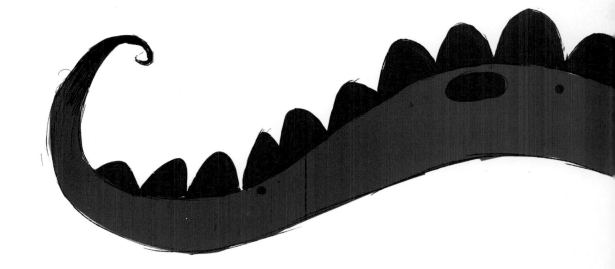

Some people love dragons; some people do not.
A boy named Nathaniel loved dragons a lot.
One night, he looked up at the glittering stars
and wondered if dragons were living on Mars.

"I'll send them an email, that's just what I'll do,
and I hope that the dragons will write to me too."
So he typed out an email, with help from his mom,
and sent it to Mars@martians.com.

Dear Dragons from Mars,

 I want you to know that I think you're the best.
Would you like to see Earth and stay here as my guest?
I know Mars is far—start packing right now!
You may get here by Tuesday
or Wednesday somehow.

Travel safely,
Nathaniel

The email was sent and the dragons received it

across millions of miles. . . . Who would have believed it!

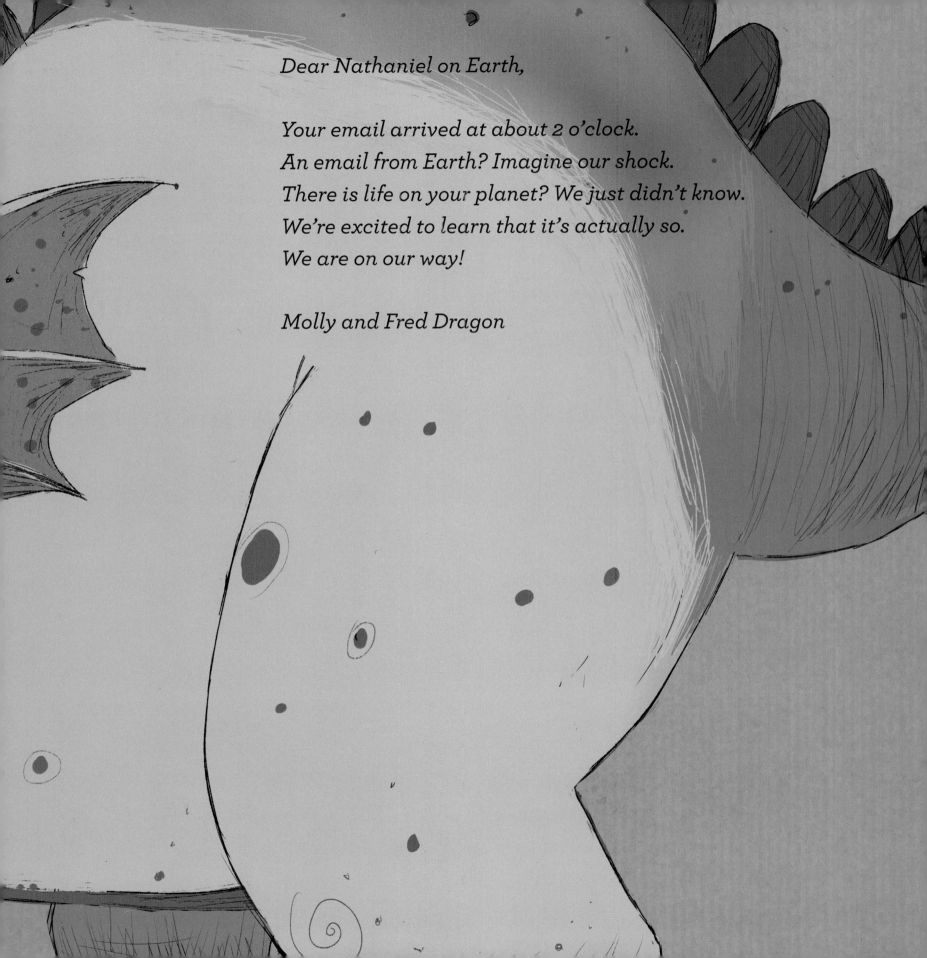

Dear Nathaniel on Earth,

Your email arrived at about 2 o'clock.
An email from Earth? Imagine our shock.
There is life on your planet? We just didn't know.
We're excited to learn that it's actually so.
We are on our way!

Molly and Fred Dragon

They packed all their things in the blink of an eye.
They were coming to Earth and were ready to fly.

Astonished, Nathaniel could only say, "Wow, my dragons are coming. . . . They're coming right now!"

Speeding past comets, they traveled for days
and landed on Earth in a fiery blaze.

Nathaniel's own mother just stood there in shock.
"Hey, Mom, aren't they great? Don't they totally rock?

Just watch them breathe fire;
just look at that plume!
Can they live in our house?
Can they stay in my room?"

"I guess it's okay,
but I'll have to require
that while in the house,
they must not breathe fire."

The dragons agreed to this difficult rule.
No flames in the house—they were totally cool.

So the dragons moved in with a leap and a bound,

a crash through the ceiling,

and trash on the ground.

The dragons were sorry they'd caused so much trouble.
Who could live in a house that was nothing but rubble?

Nathaniel again viewed the glittering stars.
Would he and his mom have to move up to Mars?
"But Mom hates to fly, so I guess that won't do.
Will Molly and Fred have to move to the zoo?"

The house was a wreck; no one could ignore it.
And Fred said to Molly, "We've got to restore it!"

So they gathered supplies,
the paint and the wood,
and repaired the whole house
the best that they could.

When the house was repaired, they did one more thing.
They added an extra-large dragon-sized wing.
The ceilings were high and the flooring was strong,
and Molly said, "Fred, this is where we belong."

Dear Martian Dragons,

We've landed on Earth in a very nice town.
Earth's our new home and we're all settled down.
Nathaniel looks after us, just like a brother.
He thinks that we're awesome, and so does his mother.
And at night when we gaze at the stars overhead,
we wish you were here!

Love,
Molly and Fred

P.S. Come visit us soon, and please bring everyone.
Earth is the planet three stops from the sun.